I0642724

John Keats is Stuck in My Butthole

And other works of literary criticism

by Wolf Larsen

Table of Contents

ABOUT WOLF LARSEN

Wolf Larsen is a comedian, writer, and poet who has traveled through over 50 countries. Wolf worked for years as a seasonal laborer in Alaska. His fiction and poetry has been published in literary magazines around the world.

Other Books by Wolf Larsen

Capitalism Sucks (non-fiction)

Honky Fucking Crazy N-Word Lover (a novel)

Pricks, Cunts, & Motherfuckers: The Novel About New York City

Eulogy for the Human Race (poems)

Pornography (poems)

Penis! Penis!! Penis!!! (a play)

Ten Thousand Penises in Your Ear (a novel)

There are many other books by Wolf Larsen to choose from. Most of Wolf's books can be purchased at online retailers.

5

John Keats is Stuck in My Butthole

Somehow, John Keats got stuck in my butthole. This might be because of the Flying saucers, or maybe the ketchup on Delicious hookers, and then of course, there is the pubic hairs of Harvard University to consider. At any rate, John Keats is currently stuck in my butthole. I can hear him screaming from my butthole:

"I am John Keats! I am So many French fries in your Logic! Actually, I'm not John Keats! I used to be John Keats, but that was Back when the solar system was created. So, if I turn back into John Keats again, put me in the primate section of the zoo, because Nuclear weapons are delicious!"

This is not the first time that John Keats has gotten stuck inside somebody's butthole. During the Toilet Paper Riots, John Keats got stuck in Shakespeare's butthole. This phenomenon is called "Bullet Hole in the butthole". Mr. Syphilis Scarface, a professor at Grab My Tits University, originally coined the name "Bullet Hole in the butthole", when he was sucking the cock of Gloria Steinem. It was in the alleyway of Boys Town when Mr. Syphilis Scarface suddenly screamed out:

"What you Crying peanut butter about? I didn't carjack no car! I was Sucking the Dick of the president of the United States of America! I borrowed this car to Deliver the Presidential Dick to Igor Stravinsky! So don't accuse me of no Carjacking!"

Of course, Shakespeare was Flying a nuclear missile to Russia when John Keats was stuck in his butthole. John Keats was also stuck in the butthole of Andy Warhol. This occurred when Brazil invaded the Circus of Nonsensical Nonsense. The learned scholar Ms. Harry Balls of Nice Round Ass University commented on this:

"I like to dress up as The world's craziest Messenger, because of All the birds in the sky smiling at me! All the birds in the sky smiling at me is the reason that I Walk around in public naked! And how come you staring at me like that? I'll eat your eyeballs if you keep staring at me like that!"

Brilliant! This is a brilliant Nice Round Ass Synopsis! Even more brilliant is the Sidewalks filled with cum stains. And why is this so brilliant? Because of the 1,000 year long vacations in Temples of Sex. And furthermore, You need a toilet plunger to discover Other solar systems. And then there's The Glory Hole of Capitol Hill, which is perhaps partly caused by Earthquakes, and this may be a factor in why John Keats is currently stuck in my butthole.

Buttholes are places where Logic is eaten by lizards. The philosophical Blue sky of buttholeism has its metaphysical origins in Pubic lice. Pubic lice being an argument for More zoos in our Insanity. Of course, Shakespeare's butthole is a place where vacations are Forever! Let's listen to Mr. Ding Dong the Third, Professor of Cunnilingus at Cocaine

University, explain Shakespeare's butthole:

"Shakespeare's butthole is a place where The Temples of Tittydom are doomed! Sometimes, in Shakespeare's bunghole Volcanic eruptions have been known to occur. This is because of The sunny skies over Toledo, Ohio. I visited Shakespeare's bunghole to research The migration of Cuckoo people with lots of cuckooism. What I found Inside of Shakespeare's butthole is Miles Davis playing rocketships blasting Off to everywhere. I think more scholarly research is necessary to find out the Gothic Goo-Goo of Shakespeare's bunghole, and also to find out if Shakespeare's butthole is sufficiently liberal & Dixiecrat to avoid being canceled."

Of course, this may have a deeper meaning of high school students dry-humping Each other . Or the deeper meaning may be A bathroom plunger stuck in the American president's butt. Either way, lots of Cubism! And lots & lots of traveling to The ears of other people. But, what Shakespeare's butthole and Wolf Larsen's butthole have in common is the Airplanes falling out of the sky . Consider the beautiful Art Deco orgies of hell, and also considering That my butt itches, and with all the Psychedelic words jingling around in my brains, one could quite clearly deduce that Jesus died with an erection. But, this is only valid when There is free parking on Sundays.

According to Ms. Mary Christmas, Professor of Lick-Lick-Lick literature at Lickety-split University, John Keats was also stuck in the butthole of Frederick Chopin. But, this was later disputed by Mr. Gobbledygook, Professor of Carjackings at the University of Yo-Yo You. Professor Gobbledygook asserts it is not possible for John Keats to have been stuck in the butthole of Frederick Chopin. Professor Gobbledygook states that:

"People getting stuck in each other's bottles is very Greek classical with lots of Insanity. Of course, whenever the Heaven of gang bangers in outer space goes Bonkers, there's a greater frequency of people getting stuck in each other's buttholes. Henry VIII got stuck inside of the butthole of Jacqueline Onassis Kennedy in this manner. It was quite a scandal for high society."

The original premise of Professor Ms. Mary Christmas is based on Monkeys scratching their balls. Meaning, it's obvious that John Keats was stuck in the butthole of Adam in the Garden of Eden, because of Flying vibrators.

Agreeing with this premises is Professor Prick Me Please, of the University of Four Letter Words, who states:

"John Keats getting stuck in the bunghole of Adam during a Nuclear war in the Garden of Eden, is regarded by some as being so Raspberry jam, but the Garden of Eden is a place where people eat God's Yummy Boogers, so I believe we should view John Keats getting stuck in the bunghole of Adam as a statement of sex & poetry & drive-by shootings. By getting stuck in the bunghole of Adam, John Keats was trying to make a statement, a statement about spray-painting Italian Renaissance orgies all over the sides of buildings."

Professor Prick Me Please thinks the reason that John Keats keeps getting stuck in other people's buttholes has something to do with The presidential debates. He calls this the Thesis of Tits. Of course, it is recognized today in academic circles that the Thesis of Tits is flawed by Herpes. This is a general consensus. A general consensus of drunks of the local bar. But, there are some who maintain that the Thesis of Tits retains validity today because of The widespread practice of people stealing each other's brains. The professor Poop A. Lot, of the Big Cock Center of the Humanities, argues that:

"Nobody can be sure who's going to get stuck in who's butthole next! This is because of Sunshine, or is it because of Musical drums going Goopy-goopity-goopity? Only the Herpes sores on our penises know the answer to this question. My own scholarly research of the past 30 years indicates that The big vagina swallowing all of outer space is here! So be ready for a complete stranger to be stuck in your butthole tomorrow morning."

Of course, not everybody agrees with Professor Poop A. Lot. John Keats affinity for getting stuck in people's bottles is regarded by some as Good-neighborly, and by others as Anti-American. But what about Train stations in our testicles? Professor Phart Moore of the Public bathroom at the Louvre seems to argue that People can't control all the solar systems flying out of their mouths. Or is that what he really is arguing?

Maybe he's arguing that Swimming across an ocean of sperm is FANTASTIC! Really? Or maybe Professor Phart Moore is arguing that You should jump into the mirror and become your own planet. Let the reader be the judge of what Professor Phart Moore is arguing:

"Napoleon Bonaparte got stuck in my wife's butthole during the Apollo mission when they were traveling to the moon together. Up on the moon, my wife observed John Keats escaping from the butthole of Isaac Newton. My wife has assisted me in my academic research regarding Ducks going quack-quack ever since, and our inquiries have produced quite a lot of Psychedelic orgies with lots of bright colors."

Such rocketships to Your childhood! Especially with all the Toilets hopping around like kangaroos! Now, the reader may be thinking that This sunshine is a communist plot to eat Flying saucers, or the reader may be thinking that Your refrigerator is talking to you in a sexy Voice, but how long until John Keats gets stuck in the reader's butthole?

A panel of Butt-fucking scholars believe that it is only a matter of time before John Keats gets stuck in the reader's butthole. This may be due to the weather . Lately, there has been lots of Sexy-sexy-sexy in the weather. This may soon change, and the weather may be very Puritanical with lots of God or political correctness. According to the experts, when the weather is very Sexy there is an increased possibility of John Keats getting stuck in the reader's butthole. Our panel of academic experts on the question of John Keats getting stuck in the reader's butthole met recently in One of Salvador Dali's paintings. These experts include the Honorable Smoking Grass, and the distinguished Doopity Dippity, his Excellency Eat Me, and a homeless man who wanted some food and a warm place to sit while we all discussed the Abstract expressionism of John Keats getting stuck in the reader's butthole.

The Honorable Smoking Grass stated:

"Buttholes in my academic lectures at the University! Lots of gargoyles in our Underwear! Satan! Satan! Satan! Satan understands our need to Perform oral sex on Wild animals! Satan understands the Thousands of horny dogs humping God's legs! I love Satan! We all love Satan!"

The homeless expert on the panel responded to this by saying: "I want some food! You guys promised me some food! Please I'm so hungry!"

These distinguished opinions regarding John Keats getting stuck in the reader's butthole shall be discussed here. First, regarding the Honorable Smoking Grass comment, I can only say that Sexy verbs hopping everywhere is very John F. Kennedy sucking-big-black-Dick. The reader may consider this Very Republican with lots of Penises running around everywhere. But what about the Leprechauns that want to be sodomized & eaten?

And then there was the comment of the homeless expert on our panel . This comment must be considered with all due academic merit. After all, Your face is very Leonardo da Vinci with lots of chili peppers! And more research may indicate that Penguins on the moon is very Toxic masculinity.

And then there was the intellectual contribution of the distinguished Doopity Dippity. The distinguished Doopity Dippity commented:

"Psychedelic Pussy to eat! Surrealistic Spermatozoa to swim in! Let's swim in Sex until we reach Another galaxy! John Keats will lead us to The wife-swapping orgies of the Garden of Eden! John Keats is our Savior of the Sexual Revolution!"

This is truly brilliant! How else can you Find somewhere to Pee? John Keats possibly getting stuck in the reader's butthole Is caused by a Field of opium growing around & around the moon. What Bazooka Of vaginas! Such sexy feet With lots of iambic pentameter! And then there's the Naked legions of sexy words!

However, I do slightly disagree with the distinguished Doopity Dippity opinion, even if it is as brilliant as Penis soup. First of all, there is the Sex-in-the-Louvre to consider . That in itself is very Outhouse painted with French Impressionist SPLAT. And second of all, Space aliens in the toilet After a number two is very nice!

And then there was the Running-naked-on-the-interstate-Highway opinion of his Excellency Eat Me. His Excellency Eat Me appears to join the scholar Suck My Lollipop, in his opinion that John Keats possibly getting stuck in the reader's butthole, is but a bunch of McDonald's

French fries. Let us read what his Excellency Eat Me said:

"McDonald's French fries served with the decapitated head of John Keats is very Skittle-your-do-Bob. Of course, sticking your Penis into the Green eggs & Ham is very 10,000-psychopaths-in-the-mirror. And eating the castrated genitals of John Keats for dessert is so Millions-of-balloons-in-the-sky."

From that statement, we can deduce that Kangaroos love homosexual Anal sex while hopping about the suburbs of America. Of course, there is always the Flowing rivers of insanity to consider . Academic research in the primate section of the zoo seems to indicate that John Keats possibly getting stuck in the reader's butthole in the future, is but a Pee-on-me-please of Plentiful happiness.

That's right! A Pee-on-me-please of Plentiful happiness.

I asked a prostitute on the street corner about the possibility of John Keats getting stuck in the reader's butthole in the future, and she, or was it a he in a dress?, I'm not really sure, what's the Planet Earth doing in the toilet?, Who's the President of the moon?, And lots of Jonestown Kool-Aid to drink.

Anyway, when asked about the possibility of John Keats getting stuck in the reader's butthole in the future, the prostitute responded:

"Once, when John Keats got stuck in the butthole of a race car driver during the Indianapolis 500, there was Crazy-spaghetti-brains-all-over-the-everything! This was very exciting for the racecar driver to have John Keats preaching the word of God in his botthole, while he was driving in fast fast speeds around & around the racecar track. He described it as The Sexiest Christian Revelation ever!"

What are we to think of this? Are we to think that a bullet in Our head is Going to save us from Horny farm animals? Or are we to think that a Transsexual George Washington on his Flying broomstick Is cumming? I let the reader be the judge.

So I jump into the mind of the reader. Inside the reader's mind is John Keats in a wedding dress getting married to the atomic bomb. Also in the reader's mind is John Keats pulling out his Dick and blessing everybody in Sunday mass with a rainbow of spermatozoa. And finally, we find in the reader's mind lots of Big

big black Dicks with sails sailing off to The lands of poetry.

So, now I the writer, and the reader, both sit down on chairs in a coffee shop in the reader's mind. Our conversation regarding the possibility of John Keats getting stuck in the reader's butthole, goes something like this:

The writer: "I use my own castrated penis as a pen."

The reader: "That sounds very 'Gone With The Wind'. Would you like some Cyanide for dessert?"

The writer: "No thanks. I Already died Today."

The reader: "Really?! Well then, Congratulations!"

The writer: "Yes. Thank you."

The reader: "Would you like some nice weather with that?"

That's when a Thousand faces of John Keats goes by...

The scholar Suck My Lollipop was also in the coffee shop that was in the reader's mind that day. The scholar Suck My Lollipop commented on this discussion:

"John Keats is very Flying-around-bananas! Without John Keats, the world would be Flat. We can thank John Keats for all the Weirdness in our normality. Of course, the Dong-Kluppy-Pippsy Empire would never have happened without John Keats. When John Keats led the Invasion of Naughty Words, John Keats saved all of academia from Boredom. We owe a lot to the Penis of John Keats."

That's when a dog in the park started to bark . The dog seemed to be commenting on the possibility of John Keats getting stuck in the reader's butthole one day. The dog seemed to be barking:

"John Keats got stuck in my butthole once. Imagine! Having the honor of John Keats getting stuck in your butthole! All the other dogs now worship me! Imagine! John Keats getting stuck in the butthole of a dog! It was the greatest day of my life!"

And then the dog made a big smelly poop. Five academics highly respected in the field of literary criticism gathered around the big smelly pile of dog poop to form an opinion. The first academic commented:

"Put some Crazy Rhythms in your Walk,
and that will cause your neighborhood to
Nincompoop the nobody! Next, add some
Adjectives-bouncing-on-the-sidewalk,
and then everything will be As cool as a
cock in the butt!"

The second academic commented on the
dog poop:

"Yippee to the Wife swapping with lots of
ketchup & mustard! I love Spray-painting
obscene murals all over The sexy walls!
Love that Pornography Spilling out of
your mouth!"

The third academic commented on the
dog poop:

"What you mean there be no jizz all over
the English language today?? I want
some Revolution in my daydreams! And I

also want some Glorious farts – and I want it now!"

And the fourth & fifth academics were too busy fucking each other up the ass to make any comment.

Now let us analyze the comments of the first three academics regarding the dog poop. Remember, the question of John Keats getting stuck in the reader's butthole in the future, is related to the issue of a big pile of dog poop in the park, by the Holy Tits of Cannibalistic Cooking. This is known as the "Take the Subway to Pornography" theory.

The comment of the first academic seems to say that the toilet paradise of The Royal Outhouse is Here! Very Blueberry orangutan! Of course, such a discourse is only possible if There are endless mouths growing everywhere.

And that is only possible if We fertilize all our dreams with John Keats's cum. (I don't care if that was grammatically correct, and if it bothers you you can eat my ass!)

Now, the comment of the second academic doesn't appear to signify any relation to John Keats possibly getting stuck in the reader's butthole one day. But this is merely a conjecture of Fornicating rabbits. More academic research regarding this question, and also the question of 10,000 gorillas in the bedroom with your wife, is necessary.

Now let's examine the third academic's comment. We can analyze the third academic's comment by Unzipping our pants and pulling out A big Kazam! This experiment will involve Transporting monks & Nuns from the Middle Ages to a whorehouse known as Capitol Hill. And we will need A time machine with lots of dildos. The result may prove the third academic's comment, but it may also disprove it.

And then there is the question of the fourth & fifth academics fucking each other up the ass. This is very significant! Because of cows falling out of the sky . And what about the Machine guns talking poetry to you? Lots of Rats crawling everywhere to talk to while you're having your Final Supper!

And then there is the phenomenon of John Keats & William Wordsworth getting stuck in each other's butts at the same time. This is both impossible & possible, because of the Bouncing-Tits-of-Timbuktu Theory. The Bouncing-Tits-of-Timbuktu Theory was developed by Your mother when she was doing academic research on Philosophy at the whorehouse. Your mother argued that Lesbian bananas are very Sunny afternoon, and that is why it's possible for John Keats & William Wordsworth to get stuck in each other's butts at the same time. Let us take a listen to Your mother at the whorehouse explaining her theory:

"This be your Lightning bolt upside the head, 'cause Your Tuna fish face ain't Santa Claus enough! You dig that Scatological noise? Because you gotta Ride that thundercloud, if you're gonna Jump on that big black Dick and surf into The nuclear Armageddon, right baby?!"

And that's the Gonorrhea of The Santa Claus Theory. However, your father taking the Empire State Building into his

little butthole in Boystown thinks that the
Gonorrhea of Santa Claus Theory is a bit
Looney Tunes, Because of all the poems
growing in the park. Your father taking it
up the ass argues that the reason that
it's possible for John Keats & William
Wordsworth to be stuck inside of each
other's butts at the same time, is not
because of the Gonorrhea of Santa Claus
Theory, but instead because of space
satellites shooting God's cum at each
other. The Gonorrhea of Santa Claus
Theory makes it possible for everyone to
be stuck in each other's butts at the
same time, argues The leprechaun with
his Empire State Building up your
father's butt. In his groundbreaking work
of literary research, "Delicious Puppy for
Caligula", The leprechaun fucking your
father Up the asS argues:

"With a certain Wild earthquake of a
personality, and without any Mouth to
speak with, I must say that Catholic
Nuns have outer space vaginas, although
there are occasions when These vaginas
turn into Squirming vowels At the
supermarket, especially On all these
Fridays that keep disappearing all the
time, but then there's Mad lobsters
grabbing your penis to consider,
especially when You forget your feet at
home, but of course there are exceptions
to this Evangelical-pussy-eating-hurrah,
like when There's too many nuclear
missiles in your Balzac, or when
Somebody's bouncing head keeps
Smashing through your window, so, what
I'm saying here, is that Chopping up
your own body into pieces and eating it
is fine, except for when The zombies in
political office cum-in-your-face, But of

course we must also think about the cum-in-your-face music found in Peanut butter jars, and the Farm tractors that keep Yelling obscenities at the fish in the ocean, and sometimes the Schoolteachers that swallow hundreds of students with their Vagina, especially when Christmas is cumming, and that's the heart of the matter."

And then there is the argument the reader made in a wet dream last night. The reader argued in his wet dream entitled "How to Become a Space Alien", that the reason it's possible for John Keats & William Wordsworth to be stuck in each other's butts at the same time, is because of Leonardo da Vinci & a thousand flying saucers crashing into each other. While he/she was having their wet dream, the reader argued:

"The monster under your bed doesn't
Suck your Dick like a kangaroo on crack-
cocaine, but Mouthfuls of cum is very
Christmas, and with all the Dogs & cats
licking your testicles, one can't help but
feel that The Cunstitution is Having an
affair with that big penis known as the
Washington Monument, and now about
the Crocodile crawling up the butthole of
the American president, the Moo-ing
moo-ing Drugs in the Brains of a cow is
very Meow meow, and that's why Toe
licking tastes like escargot, and I
presume that Alleyways full of piss &
cum is really liberty & justice for all, just
as my colleagues might Exchange wives
with the Primates in the zoo, and now for
the Orchestra of Clitorus at Symphony
Hall, which, by the way, is impossible
without Dr. Seuss showing up in drag,
but butthole to him!, and that's why

Nuclear missiles in my Balzac will send lots of philosophy your way, yes, I'm quite sure of it. And lots of Sexy helicopters Too!"

Now, apparently the reader has no recollection of making this argument. And this in itself is possible because of Your wife jumping into a time machine and making love to all the monks of the Middle Ages. Professor Crack Head commented on cities that sail past our imaginations, that this indeed makes it possible to join a discussion about John Keats & William Wordsworth being stuck in each other's butts, while having a wet dream, and having no recollection of said discussion. Professor Crack Head also argues that outer space is made out of circus clown jism. Let us take a listen to Professor Crack Head in his work

"Pornographic Academia for Horny Lizards":

"Go fuck your mother you Imbecile of Imbeciles! You're a Big strawberry on two legs, and you're a Spy for the rats in the sewers, and you're also a Screwdriver penis without a Blue sky! I hope you Get eaten by a puppy! I wouldn't waste my diarrhea on you! So go Jump back in your mother's Vagina!"

The reader is not the only person to join the discussion about John Keats & Williams Wordsworth being stuck in each other's butts while having a wet dream. Another person who joined this discussion while having a wet dream is That guy on the subway train talking to himself. Their opinion regarding John Keats & Williams Wordsworth being stuck in each other's butts, seems to be That squirrels in the park are spying on us for space alien civilizations, but That guy talking to himself on the subway train only holds this opinion on rainy days. On sunny days, That guy talking to himself on the subway train holds the opinion that Medieval painting would be impossible without frog jism. This is very Upstairs for a Horny sexy wife with a stranger. Its connection to John Keats & Williams Wordsworth being stuck in each other's butts, is very Billions of people melting into the poetry. We must also consider Tornadoes of female orgasms Roaring across the land...

This brings up the subject of the wet dreams of John Keats. The cashier at your local supermarket, the foremost expert on the wet dreams of John Keats, argues that the wet dreams of John Keats are symbolic of squirrel testicles.

The cashier at your local supermarket in her celebrated academic work "Chlamydia Monsters for You" also argues that blow jobs in heaven is very Michelangelo with a touch of Elbow grease. The relationship here to the wet dreams of John Keats is very Falling bombs everywhere. The reader will see this relationship in this passage of "Chlamydia Monsters for You":

"Outer space with All your accusations! Lots of pink flamingos with your Face! Naughty With vroom vroom all the time! And sexy sexy Shit smeared all over your naked body all the time! Penis! Lots of orgies in the Hallways of Heaven! Toilet!"

As groundbreaking as this opinion is regarding the wet dreams of John Keats, this opinion is not shared by all academics. Professor Wet Panties of

McDonald's Hamburgers University has a very different opinion about the wet dreams of John Keats. Professor Wet Panties seems to argue that The happiness of our buttocks is dependent on Delicious puppy with fried fireflies. Or is he arguing that Birds are really space aliens? Let the reader be the judge. Here we quote Professor Wet Panties:

"Hey reader! What's your Upside down? Hey reader! How come All the American presidents are jammed up your butt? Hey reader! Give me your Thoughts with barbecue sauce! Hey reader! We're going to Alice in Wonderland on crack together! That's right! So much now! So much psYchOpaThiC-maSs-shOOtiNg-arT cooking in our brains! This is so Screeching television sets for all the barking dogs!"

Doesn't this seem very Toilet in the brains? I wonder if I'm the only one that finds this point of view very Lovely with STDs. Others find Professor Wet Panties' point of view not Lovely with STDs at all. Instead, they find Professor Wet Panties' point of view as being very Sunny afternoon. Only An astronaut taking a shit into outer space would know . This is because when John Keats was a NASA astronaut, The planet Earth had been hidden by a squirrel under a tree in the park. A bird flying by commented:

"The fires of hell feels so beautiful! The fires of Literature bellowing out of John Keats's butthole Are positively Delicious pussy! Upon examining the fires of Literature bellowing out of John Keats' butthole, we find that The killer whales & dolphins swimming out of your pussy are very... And then there is the Graffiti art inside of each butthole that John Keats has visited. This is very Sexy to your dog, and appears to be related to Cat Sex symphonies at 3 in the morning. Further academic research is necessary to find out how this relates to John Keats riding a nuclear missile from This book into the poetry of Anne Sexton."

Before I could ask the bird's position in academia, he Pooped a bunch of academic jargon on me and flew away. Academics have analyzed the bird shit that fell on my head, and believe that this is related to the scatological experiences of John Keats.

Professor 10,000 Psychopaths-in-Your-Closet, the world's most renowned scholar on the scatological experiences of John Keats, has often argued that Pelicans can swallow whole entire solar systems. However, on other occasions he has argued that Prostitute pussy is Filled with philosophy. Here's what Professor 10,000 Psychopaths-in-Your-Closet has to say about the scatological experiences of John Keats:

"What Space alien literature can be found in our buttholes? That is the question! It is a question of The words on this page fornicating with each other for all eternity. Or is it a question of Thousands & thousands of hotel rooms filled with all kinds of kinky sex stretching our imaginations to the limits of the universe? Lots of Cock Boys of Satan for everybody! But what is special about the butthole of John Keats is how it delivers us to other universes beyond this one."

Isn't this very Michelangelo's David wiping his ass with both the Democratic & Republican platforms? Professor Fook My Wife seems to think so . Professor Fook My Wife, at a seminar entitled "Wife Sharing With Space Aliens", argued that the scatological experiences of John Keats were very Babbling-&-babbling-suns-in-the-sky. That is, when they weren't Masturbating to the guillotine going up and down. This is known as the Man sitting on the toilet giving speeches about Scatology to the general public. Professor Fook My Wife stated at the seminar:

"The mystery of the butthole of John Keats is very Historical. And why does John Keats always visit the buttholes of other people? Is this an interplanetary butthole visiting Human civilization? Or is this a philosophical journey to discover the Existentialism in our buttholes? I will present to you a hypothesis that John Keats is really a Porn actor from the Italian Renaissance, and that he visits other people's buttholes as part of a journey of poetry. Because every butthole is filled with poetry!"

Of course, Both John Keats & Salvador Dali attended the Scatological University of Saturn's Rings together. And they were both impressed with each other's scatological abilities. One of their professors was A Giant Penis. A Giant Penis commented that both students possessed a unique quality of Eating out all the vaginas of the primates at the zoo. A Giant Penis thought that John Keats scatological abilities were quite Divine. And A Giant Penis considered the scatological abilities Of Salvador Dali to be As learned as Your dog. Your dog in his groundbreaking book on scatological studies entitled "American Democracy for Sale" states that:

"John Keats and Salvador Dali each has a unique butthole. The bunghole of John Keats can only be described as being Full of butterflies. Whereas, the bunghole of Salvador Dali is The favorite hiding place of The Mayor of Chicago. This difference between the buttholes of John Keats & Salvador Dali affected the Apollo mission to the moon, because of McDonald's hamburgers. McDonald's hamburgers is the unifying Piano Concerto of Farts in the buttholes of John Keats & Salvador Dali. The differences & similarities in the buttholes of John Keats & Salvador Dali presents us with a contradiction. This contradiction is very Fishy like tasty Vagina, and can only be resolved with

Sailing off to Some story in the Old Testicle of the Bible."

This is so Drunken parrots screeching Obscene prophecies! The premise of this Avalanche of Rolling testicles is that scatologicaly John Keats is so very Creative, and Salvador Dali is Full of Dreams flying through the desert sands...

Of course, the well-known Harry Vagina of Venice disagrees. The Harry Vagina of Venice believes that John Keats & Salvador Dali are very Religious, scatologicaly speaking. And scatologicaly speaking, the main difference between John Keats & Salvador Dali is that Keats is 10,000 geese flying out of the penis of Christ as he dies on the cross.

What are we to make of this Fairytale of Porn actors in the Garden of Eden? In commenting on the thesis of The Harry Vagina of Venice, Professor Genital Warts disagrees with the premise of Delicious puppies flying into your mouth from the Land of Oz. Professor Genital Warts believes that John Keats & Salvador Dali are very similar, scatologicaly speaking, except for Train tracks that lead to The beginning of time...

This brings up the question of how John Keats ended up in the microwave oven of Wolf Larsen. And what is the answer? One of the farts of John Keats believes the answer lies in dancing-big-buttocks & more dancing-big-buttocks & more dancing-big-buttocks. Of course, it is well-known that the right armpit of John Keats has a different theory. Let us listen to the right armpit of John Keats explain to us the Marching Craziness of

Yesterdays stomping & stomping around us:

"As the right armpit Of John Keats, I am fully aware that All stairways lead to Smelly vaginas full of psychedelic art. But does the reader realize that the butthole of John Keats is a place where Artists have gathered for centuries? And has the reader considered that the reason that John Keats lives in the buttholes of other people is connected to the Aurelia Barelas (Northern lights)? I would summarize these 10 Commandments of Nose Picking with the following phrase: Worship thy Penis! And there you have it!"

When the right armpit of John Keats published this opinion in the Journal of Jacking Off, the left armpit of John Keats wrote a contrary opinion, which was also

published in the Journal of Jacking Off.
Let us see what the left armpit of John
Keats has to say about People boarding
ships to The psychedelic 1960s:

"People boarding ships to the Psychedelic
1960s? What jisms of art exploding
everywhere! What Wrecking balls of
rebellion! If people are going to board
ships to The psychedelic 1960s, then
what will happen to our traditional values
of Intergalactic nipples? And what is to
become of our religion of Immaculate
conceptioning the right hand & the Penis
every afternoon? Only John Keats can
save us from The puritanical Crocodile
tears of Lemon meringue pie! John Keats
for President!"

When this opinion was published in the
highly respectable Journal of Jacking Off,
the left testicle of John Keats published a

contrary opinion in the Journal of Mass Shootings. As the reader probably knows, the left testicle of John Keats is one of the most foremost experts on Beastility. Let us examine closely the Dancing-big-buttocks opinion of the left testicle of John Keats:

"As the left testicle of John Keats, I have much insight into Erotic rituals with farm animals. Now, John Keats was a practicing member of the Royal Beastility Society, and as an outstanding member of the Royal Beastility Society, John Keats practiced great Sexual democracy in the animal kingdom! And for his services of Sexual democracy in the animal kingdom, John Keats was awarded the John F. Kennedy Prize of Beastity By the Prince of Swallowing Cum. I hope that future generations will appreciate the great services that John

Keats provided to the animal kingdom, and advancing the great cause of beastility."

While this opinion was much applauded by the pubic hairs of John Keats, the pubic hairs of Marie Antoinette had some strong disagreements with the statement. The pubic hairs of Marie Antoinette seemed to think that the pubic hairs of John Keats were very Enlightened on this question, But the pubic hairs of Marie Antoinette had their disagreements nonetheless with the pubic hairs of John Keats. After all, the pubic hairs of Marie Antoinette are most learned on the subject of The love affairs of German shepherds with women of high society. Let us listen to the pubic hairs of Marie Antoinette:

"When I had sex with John Keats, I found the pubic hairs of John Keats to be very learned on a variety of subjects, including the subject of Sexy food for cannibalistic delights. My pubic hairs & the pubic hairs of John Keats would discuss so many issues of the day, including Penises crashing into impressionist art. Yes, I do believe that the pubic hairs of John Keats will be considered some of the most intellectual pubic hairs of all time!"

Despite their mutual admiration, The pubic hairs of John Keats published a rebuttal to the fundamental ideas of the pubic hairs of Marie Antoinette. This rebuttal was published on The buttocks of All the capitalist politicians, and was read by All the whores in the red light district. Everyone reading this rebuttal suddenly Had sex with each other. All I can say about the matter is that The herpes on my penis are very glad to meet you. The butthole of Benjamin Franklin commented:

"As the butthole of Benjamin Franklin, I feel that it is very important for patriotic Americans to understand the great contributions that John Keats made to Smelly crotches everywhere. Without these contributions of the great intellect of John Keats' butthole, the United States of America would not be the great nation it is today. So please, all Americans, raise the flagpoles between your legs in honor of the great intellect of John Keats's butthole, and to its great contributions to posterity."

Naturally, the butthole of John Keats disagreed. The butthole of John Keats is so very very Highly cultured, that

Dolphins swim in it. So it seems natural that the butthole of John Keats & Benjamin Franklin would disagree on the question of Dick-me-all-night-long and Dick-me-all-night-long and Dick-me-all-night-long. However, the buttholes of John Keats & Benjamin Franklin do agree that angels from heaven are very sexy. But why is this so? A man walking outside naked right now seems to feel that this agreement is due to Forests of schizophrenia growing in your thoughts. However, a different academian, the Magician of Masturbation, seems to feel that this agreement between the butthole of John Keats & Benjamin Franklin has to do with Sex robots sodomizing Jesus Christ. Let us take a listen to The Magician of Masturbation explaining more on this matter:

"To sodomize Jesus Christ, or not to sodomize Jesus Christ? That is the question! When John Keats & Benjamin Franklin & a horde of sex robots sodomized Jesus Christ, it was a great day of Gonorrhea. In fact, let me say it was a wonderful day of Wackiness for all of humanity! Three cheers to John Keats & Benjamin Franklin & that horde of sex robots for sodomizing Jesus Christ, and furthering human civilization by doing so!"

So should we give each other the Nobel Prize for Sexually Transmitted Diseases? Or Should we all just Eat each other out? Currently, John Keats (who is still stuck in the author's butthole) is whispering to me via The Intergalactic Butthole Machine, that The homoerotic Jesus & his transvestite disciples is Very sexy with whipped cream. Now, this might seem an

obvious answer to Global warming, but
what exactly does it all mean?

Did Shakespeare Have a Big Black Dick?

Scholars have been debating for quite some time whether Shakespeare had a big black Dick? Was Shakespeare black? Or was Shakespeare a space alien? Or was Shakespeare a sex robot? And even if Shakespeare was black, that doesn't necessarily mean that he had a big Dick. But that also begs the question, did Shakespeare have a nice ass?

These are the burning questions that academics have wanted to know ever since Albert Einstein took his first shit. At the University of Albert Einstein Taking a Shit, some scientists of The public toilet have even suggested that Shakespeare

was an Italian transported to England via
Adolf Hitler's testicles. Or was
Shakespeare a Jew from New York City
transported to Mars via Television? And
even if Shakespeare were white,
Shakespeare could have acquired a big
black Dick from His stockbroker. This
was a very common practice back in
Neanderthal Mars. Let us consider the
point of view of Professor Dirty Tennis
Shoes of Spank Me University:

"So crazy with Your brains burning and
burning! So Tarzan with Lots of smelly
underwear! So smelly vagina with lots of
Groovy polkadots! So tits With so much
Washington DC! The time for Lots of
Washington DC tits is now! And now is
the big Arena of thousands of hookers!
So take out your penis – and create lots
of Art with your penis! Now is the time!
Let's Find some new insanity to create!"

After reading that, the reader may be wondering about New York City rats in his bed at night. After all, New York City rats in your bed Tonight would affect What happened yesterday, and that would be a determining factor if Shakespeare had a big black Dick. If Shakespeare had a big black Dick, then We should all praise God! Professor Three Testicles of Blabity Blabity Blabity University, believes the question of Shakespeare's big Dick is related to a man with a giant mouth eating thousands of puppies every hour. And in addition, is Shakespeare related to that Dick Cheney? After all, Shakespeare was a Porn actor. And that Dick Cheney was also a Porn actor. Absolute proof that both Shakespeare & that Dick Cheney were Playing golf with a giant penis together. This has been substantiated by the following passage from "The Wet Panties of the Virgin Mary" written by Marie Antoinette after she was decapitated:

"We yes to Lots of rainbows! We no to All these clothes Holding us back from the full expression of nudity! So much testicles to hear the birds sing! So many arrows flying all over the world from our penises! Peace & joy to our penises! Peace & joy to our vaginas!"

Marie Antoinette seems to imply here that Penises can slither their way to other planets. But how does this relate to Shakespeare's big black Dick? And how does it relate to Alleyways of Crazy? The President of the United States with his clothes off sees the relationship here as one of Your-brains-Rotting-like-fruit, because after all Shakespeare's big black

Dick would be Extraterrestrial, and this would entail Medieval England being invaded by flying testicles from outer space, but only if The Virgin Mary sang All the Oh-oh-oh ah-ah-ah of immaculate conception, in which case I lost all my spermatozoa in other woman's vaginas, and that's why If you keep reading this you'll get herpes. The herpes on Shakespeare's penis was first noticed by the distinguished Janitor of the American President's butthole. The distinguished janitor of the President's butthole has been studying Shakespeare's big Dick for thousands of years. The studies of This distinguished janitor seems to indicate that Shakespeare's big black Dick may have been involved in Trafficking a bunch of naughty naughtiness. However, if Shakespeare's big black Dick was involved in Trafficking a bunch of naughty naughtiness, then how does one explain Insanity splashing down the streets? Here to explain the Beautiful insanity of Shakespeare's big Dick is the Grand Academian of the Fireflies Ms. Hairiest Pussy on Earth:

"With fireflies we can change the sky! My nipples are telling you I love you! My bellybutton is telling you lots of daydreams! My bouncing buttocks are telling you endless wisdom! And the sunshine is telling you so much sensuality. So let's swim inside our testicles!"

But what about Going insane with as many people as you can find? And how does the Coming nuclear war relate to Shakespeare's big black Dick? Because if Shakespeare's big black Dick was playing Beethoven's Sixth Symphony, then wouldn't this cause The reader to Be swallowed by a goldfish? Or would Shakespeare's big black Dick cause traffic jams on other planets? And is Shakespeare's big black Dick going to run for President of the United States of America? And what is the Extraterrestrial intelligence of Shakespeare's big black Dick anyway? Here to answer these questions is the Academic Barking Dog of Kalamazoo on Mars:

"Grasshoppers be hopping into the Toilet paper Armageddon, and this is causing Shakespeare's big black Dick to debate philosophy with All the Greek philosophers in Boystown! But with The neoconservative politics of Shakespeare's big black Dick, one can only jack off thousands of chickens! Gazooks to the Plants & trees drunk on sunlight! Invade the Minds of the space aliens! Let's fry ourselves in The cooking juices ejaculating out of Shakespeare's big black Dick! If only there was more Cooking juices ejaculating out of Shakespeare's big black Dick!"

But how could this be true, if Shakespeare's big Dick is Being auctioned off at Christie's? And if Shakespeare's big black Dick is auctioned off at Christie's, then how does one explain the Train crashes? After all, Train crashes with English grammar could only occur if Shakespeare had a little Dick. But if Shakespeare's Dick was little, was it still black? Let us listen to Mr. Itchy Back, of the Institute of Mooing Cows:

"With all the Clones of Shakespeare's big black Dick suddenly hanging from the crotches of white men, The reader will inevitably Go crazy with all the sunlight.

This is So much strawberries to you, isn't it?! So why Dance naked through the steel mills with all your ancestors? With so much Nakedness pouring out of these words, there will be Millions & billions of big Shakespeare black Dicks growing out of the ground tomorrow. And now All the metaphysical aspects of Shakespeare's big black Dick will be visible to the eyes of grasshoppers on the moon. Maybe We should Hallucinate ourselves into new places? So, create a big Interplanetary crashing of all the everything in the universe with Angry computer codes! Your fingers dancing with madness on the computer dashboard, now?"

Of course, when Beethoven played with Shakespeare's big black Dick it was very Romantic. And when Mozart played with Shakespeare's big black Dick it was very Thousands of whores everywhere. And when Bella Bartok played with Shakespeare's big Dick it was very Catastrophic with disco dancing. At least, that is the view of the eminent Blip-Flip-Plip, of the Anal Warts Institute for the Studies of Pussy Juices. Let us examine the glorious rantings & ravings of the eminent Blip-Flip-Plip:

"For us to Become one with the eternity, we must be aware of The imposters of Shakespeare's big black Dick, and that entails Mind-traveling to the faraway lands of Your mother's pussy, of which only a Guru of Trash Cans can know. And now for the Scrambled eggs Of meditating On a big pair of plastic boobs. This is so Crowded sidewalks of sPaCe-aLieN-ciTieS! So Lots of shotgun blasts! So yippie-ya-yes to midnight masturbations! TootaLou?"

This opinion is not shared by your neighbor living upstairs, who is Professor Crazy of the Duck Quacking. Professor Crazy felt that Beethoven's rendition of Shakespeare's big black Dick was more Thousands of screaming monsters in an outhouse. He also felt that Crooked-politicians-swimming-into-your-ears is the dominating factor in Mozart's Concerto for Shakespeare's Big Black Dick. However, this opinion is not shared by other academians. Professor Banana Peel of the Sidewalk commented:

"As a sidewalk magician of the utmost Lunacy, I can only say that the phenomenon of Shakespeare's big black Dick is so Country music with Gunshots, that we all must be line-dancing with Our murderers before they kill us! Yes! We all absolutely must Jump into the mouths Of grizzly bears and land in their bellies!

And now, for my next trick I shall Steal the North American continent!"

Picasso's painting of Shakespeare's big Dick is famous for its oinking pigs. And Renoir's painting of Shakespeare's big Dick is Happy with too much pussy. In contrast, Rembrandt's painting of Shakespeare's big Dick is widely regarded as more Elephants-riding-unicycles-around-your-apartment. Examined closely, these paintings of Shakespeare's big black Dick are symbolic of Feminists & born-again Christians with rabies, or at least, that is the view held by Professor Lunatic Asylum of His Merry Moopa:

"What Saturn's rings with black Shakespeare Dick! What Big black Dick with Geography lessons from a big pair of tits! It's time for The July 4th celebrations of Shakespeare's big black Dick! Run like a Big black Dick on crack-cocaine! Make Crack-cocaine your religion while Shakespeare's big black Dick is pummeling your asshole with Zen Buddhism! Unmake all that has ever been made! Search for The big testicles of the universe! And now discover the Zen Buddhism of Sitting on the toilet of God's face!"

Professor Marquis de Sade of The Devil's Pleasure Dungeon, on the other hand, argues that Shakespeare's Dick was black, but that Shakespeare himself was white. Professor Marquis de Sade states that the obvious reason for this is "Elephants on-unicycles getting stuck in the reader's colon". But later, Professor Marquis de Sade came to disagree with his earlier position, and came to believe that Shakespeare was a Jew with a space alien Dick. Professor Marquis de Sade argued that Shakespeare was a Jew with a space alien Dick because of "Street-corners-rolling-around-with-mental-illness". But then, this brings up the question of eyeballs in the toilet looking up at you after you take a number two. In addition, there is Oversexed sheep visiting you at all hours of the day & night to consider, especially with Rocketships to the whorehouse, and the Insane people that keep-walking-into-your-mind, and that is why I be jumping up to the clouds, except when I lose my feet in the whorehouse or City Hall or someplace like that, and when That happens on a WHAM BAM Friday, and It's a Friday filled with fornicating corpses, when the Procreating words are so yippee! This is the view held by the Psycho Gorilla Pyromaniacs of the

Academic Group of Groupies. At their Conference of Booty Hole Inspections the members of this academic group argued that:

"No one can quite Disappear To another universe fast enough! That's because Shakespeare's big black Dick is a telescope that can see into outer space! Can the reader see all the Fireflies singing With big black Dick around him? Of course you can! That's because The streets are slobbering with Pussy juices from a pussycat! And can the readers see all the vaginas slobbering around him?"

The reader may be thinking: how is this possible? If Shakespeare indeed had a space alien's Dick, how did Shakespeare obtain this space alien Dick, And how does this relate to That gang-bang your mother had 9 months before you were born? These are questions brought up by a store mannequin that lives inside a book at the library. The store manikin argues that you have to be boo-doo-dippy to be Up north of Shakespeare's big black Dick, right? However, this opinion is contradicted by The reader's mother, who states that "lots of WOW-WOW! Strange Nonsense is happening every Time you look around in your mind!" This hypothesis seems to negate the other hypothesis concerning the origins of Shakespeare's Dick, which may in fact be A delicious recipe for dying. But if Shakespeare's Dick is A delicious recipe for dying, then what about street corners running everywhere? Here to shed light on this question is A corpse laying in the street, who stated in their groundbreaking theoretical work "I Have an Interesting Tattoo on My Butt" that:

"It's so Strawberry juice and wild with Obscene tattoos running all over everybody's skin! I have dived into Obscenity and found The Heaven of Anuses where Shakespeare's big black Dick will live happily ever after! And once I found The Heaven of Anuses, The orgies of dogs & cats was bound to happen!"

Yet, how is this possible if Your brains are melting inside your head? Richard Pryor, when he was interviewing Shakespeare about his supposedly big black Dick, said that "The new extraterrestrial languages feel so good up the butt!". This seems to prove that Shakespeare was actually Asian, but that he did indeed have a big black Dick. An astronaut in outer space commented that it is possible for an Asian to have a big black Dick, because of the Phoo Fum Fickle Factor. However, My Athlete's Foot argues that the Phoo Fum Fickle Factor would only apply if Shakespeare were a black man with a vagina. So was Shakespeare a black man with a big hairy vagina? Virginia Woolf, in her novel "Eat My Nasty Pussy" seems to allude to a William Shakespeare with a big hairy vagina. Here is a passage from Virginia Woolf's novel "Eat My Nasty Pussy":

"So the man was walking into a Thousand grains of insanity. The person behind the counter was Not a person. This caused All the planets of the universe to get lost and End up in your closet. Once the person behind the counter Suddenly became a sculpture, the room became a tornado. The tornado of the room sang thousands of voices of Madness. This saved the world from Being boring."

Everyone knows that Virginia Woolf herself had a big black Dick. This was established by Winston Churchill, when Winston Churchill was A hustling male prostitute in Times Square. But if Virginia Woolf had a big black Dick, and Shakespeare was a black man with a big hairy vagina, then What happened to daylight Savings time? Daylight Savings time is rightly regarded as Nuns with giant strap-ons raping all of Santa's elves, as all Nuns with giant strap-ons are The Mistresses of Oversexed Donkeys, and all of Santa's elves are The Lords of Lunacy, and all Sexy school teachers are all imaginary beings from the mind of A robot. However, what about Immaculate conception with a donkey? Some theoreticians think that William Shakespeare did not have just one Harry vagina, but that Shakespeare possessed three Harry vaginas in between his legs. Professor Yapping Chihuahua of the Loo at the Louvre argues that the three vaginas of Shakespeare were Flying saucers, and that this was normal for Tuesday, and certainly not a Subway train stuck in your butt. In her address to the Crispy Cunt Convention Professor Yapping Chihuahua explained:

"No one is Living on the planet Earth anymore, because everyone is Shakespeare's big black Dick! And when we understand this Forever with Lunacy all over it, then ecstasy always happens! Always always happens the Ecstasy! You see?"

Some people think that Shakespeare was not a human at all. They think he was a dog With the head of a giraffe. Professor Buttocks of Buttville argues that "You pick up your Bible of Shakespeare's Big Black Dick, and you create new visions of Crack-cocaine festivals with it".

And that is why Shakespeare was a Ham sandwich, which was eaten by A killer whale that was swimming between your ears. But let us examine this question with lots of Diarrhea from the butt of a butt monster. After all, if Shakespeare was a dog, then Question marks bouncing around in your testicles are bound to happen. And if Shakespeare was a dog, did he still have a big black Dick? Here to illuminate us on this loud question is Two cats noisily fucking in the alleyway below your window at three in the morning, who tell us that "We wear our Eyeballs all over our thoughts, because of All this poetry galloping out of Shakespeare's big black Dick".

So, if Shakespeare was a dog with a Big Black Dick, Then it follows that Penis is delicious with 1960s decor. But this has been called into question by the Conference of Penis Eaters, which collectively came to the conclusion that Black men in dresses are really hot. So, then it follows that, Shakespeare was actually a Sex robot Who followed Jesus Christ around Jerusalem, and he did not have a big black Dick at all, instead he had Cambridge University between his legs, So his crotch was very learned. A little boy playing with his wee wee writes in the Journal of Jacking Off:

"I am more frustrated than a Camel from the desert stuck on a spaceship! I tried to take a shit, but then The giant city happened! And my naked mother jumped out of the toilet, and wanted to have sex with me! So I suddenly became one of the men on the Sistine Chapel painted by Michelangelo. I was as shocked as a Dog being flown out to outer space, but that's A thousand years before Your father shot his worthless dickweed into your mother!"

Of course, when you add lots of naughty Sex with 90-year-old nuns to this argument, you get Highways of flying words. And that brings into question the origins of Shakespeare's big black Dick. Perhaps the origins of Shakespeare's big black Dick was Socrates & Plato, back when they worked at a McDonald's during the night shift together. Or perhaps the origins of Shakespeare's Dick was Hundreds of flying saucers flying out of your mother's vagina. Here to debate this question is Professor 7,000 Years of Herpes, who believes that Shakespeare's big black Dick was a Gothic Phenomena Experienced by Edgar Allan Poe in a public bathroom. However, Professor Zop Bop Cock disagrees, and believes that Shakespeare's big black Dick was caused by A thunderstorm on the planet of Jupiter. Professor Switch Blade and Professor Up-Down-Up-Down debated this question at the Harvard School of Defecation, in front of an audience of Screaming genitals. The results of this debate was Frogs-hopping-everywhere. The debate about Shakespeare's big black Dick brought up questions, such as What should we have for breakfast? Should we have big black Dick for breakfast? And what about the Monstrous sun that's swallowing us all with its big yellow rays? And how about Attaching thousands of big brightly-colored boobs to all of the skyscrapers? A Dead corpse 10 feet under the ground commented to A flying saucer in the sky:

"The thousands of Siamese twins in your picnic basket are always screaming their politics at you. But this is very Delicious meatballs with delicious human eyeballs. It will be replaced by Shakespeare's big black Dick on a plate of spaghetti & marinara sauce. So, I'll see you soon at the Butcher shop of human meat!"

A dog at the park argued that Shakespeare had a black Dick, but it was a small black Dick. Of course, black nationalists everywhere deny that it is possible for a black Dick to be small. However, this dog (and it was a dog with four legs) claimed to have had a sexual relationship with Shakespeare, and that is how he became acquainted with the size of Shakespeare's Dick. Interviewing the dog was The President of France. The President of France has been studying Shakespeare's Dick since All that abracadabra. Anyway, The President of France also interviewed a declawed gerbil who claimed to have had a sexual relationship with Shakespeare as well. The declawed gerbil was less familiar with Shakespeare's Dick, and more familiar with Shakespeare's anus. So we can disregard this Gerbil-in-the-butt. However, what about the Political views of Shakespeare's Big black Dick? Was Shakespeare's private parts part of the Eat Me Empire? In his groundbreaking study On the culinary uses of cum, Professor Cum-a-Lot said that Shakespeare's private parts were

86

"Symbolic of the Christmas spirit." However, if that is true, then how do we explain Being swallowed by All this chaos? There is also the additional question of What mass murder would look good With Those shoes? Professor Sex-a-Lot of Chlamydia University helps shed some much needed light on this question of Shakespeare's private parts:

"First there are the pussys of Time travel! And then there are the pussys of Intergalactic fun! But very Artistic, are the pussys of The future!"

So, from this quoted passage above it follows That everyone should drink yellow water out of the public toilet. Yet, how do we explain the Herpes Sores growing all over Shakespeare's Dick, whether it was black or not, and whether it was big or not, The burning question of the herpes sores on Shakespeare's Dick has been puzzling academics since *bu*B*blegU*m-*bU*bb*Legu*M-*bu*B*bl*E*gu*M. This is very Delicious worms, as the herpes sores on Shakespeare's Dick were known to be very Scrambled eggs & drive-by-shootings, according to Professor Nobody. Professor Nobody argues that the herpes sores on Shakespeare's Dick were part of a process of Ka-BOOM, and should be viewed with much Celebration Of Cockdom, but only if Itch-itch-itch-itch-itch, as long as we take in consideration all of the Flying everything. This will of course infinitely help our further understanding of the herpes on Shakespeare's big Black Dick.

Yet, what if instead of having Herpes sores on his big black Dick, Shakespeare had A monastery of hundreds of monks living on his big black Dick. The

Department of Dippity Duda at The
garbage dump outside town has been
studying this possibility since The reader
was born. Your grandmother on LSD,
who has been a Sex slave of the
Department of Dippity Duda since yippie-
dippy-lollipop, argues that WHOOPIE!
Therefore, it follows that there may have
been Lots of graffiti art painted on
Shakespeare's big black Dick. However,
what about Having sex with dead
people? The Journal of Artsy-Fartsy
Scatology sheds an interesting light on
this puzzling question:

"The toilets of space aliens are very
Exciting! And that's why we've been
studying the toilets of space aliens for a
very long time. The toilets of space
aliens can answer questions about Who's
having sex with who. But the toilets of
space aliens are also very dangerous,

because of The landscapes of Art all around that keep on swallowing people!"

Therefore, it follows that Psychotic penguins love the reader! Of course, because if Shakespeare has a big black Dick, then Probably all the nuns in the Catholic Church have big black Dix between their legs too. But if Shakespeare has a small black Dick, then Everybody should have tattoos of The periodic table of elements On their buttocks. This is called the Fellatio Factor Of The bLow job Factory. A sexy midget of the Sexy Midget Institute for the Advancement for Sex of Midgets, has studied the Fellatio Factor Of Blow jobism ever since The dinosaurs invaded New York City. If Shakespeare has a small black Dick, then Cannibalism is sexy. Sexy sexy cannibalism is related to the Sexy Sexy Midget Syndrome, which is related to the Bonk Bonk Bonk Question, which is connected to the Birds singing outside. The sexy midget comments:

"You been here to see this?! You gotta see this Voyage to The crazy of the crazy that's just so crazy! And there's lots of Shakespeare's big black Dicks flying all around! Big black Dicks flying in the air! You gotta jump on your Speeding phrase-of-poetry, and come see this Voyage to So much crazy!"

This is a big voilà with lots of Sexy adjectives to bonk me bonk me bonk me with! Or maybe, it is a small voilà with lots of Bank robberies. Either way, it brings into question if Shakespeare stole his big black Dick from Winston Churchill. Winston Churchill (interviewed at the graveyard in a podcast for dead people) claims that Shakespeare stole his big black Dick on the Night of Naughty. A witness to these proceedings of the theft of this big black Dick that came into the possession of Shakespeare, however, was not found. Much scholarly work has been written regarding whether Shakespeare stole his big black Dick from Winston Churchill. But if Shakespeare stole his big black Dick from somebody else, then how come Adolf Hitler had a little penis? Furthermore, there is lots of Caviar in Marilyn Monroe's pussy to consider. (Eat that caviar!) Like, what if Flying saucers from outer space invaded Marilyn Monroe's pussy to eat that Caviar? And if That happened, then it follows that Shakespeare's big black Dick may have come from The Cambodian dictator Pol Pot. This is precisely what Mozart-being-fucked-up-the-ass-by-a-big-gorilla-at-the-zoo argues in their book "Musical Testicles". Mozart-being-fucked-up-the-ass-by-a-big-gorilla-at-the-zoo argues that "Musical testicles is the reason that God went insane!" Let's examine this idea, and its relationship to the big black Dick of Shakespeare. A man pissing in the alleyway outside claims that there is confusion between the big black Dick of Jesus Christ, and the big black Dick of Shakespeare. But where does this confusion come from? According to The man pissing in the alleyway outside, this confusion comes from The reader's first orgasm. In their doctoral thesis in the Pee on Yourself Program at the University of Bop Hopp & Klopp, The man pissing in the alleyway outside states that:

"Sometimes with all the Brains jumping out of our heads, I find myself

Masturbating with all the birds in the sky, but this only causes Buildings to melt all over me, and then Too much kamikazee happens, which I can't really control, because of all the Nuclear missiles in the clown's butt, but I'm doing my best to Become a child again, because after all, Shakespeare's big black Dick is creating children all over the world!"

But what does this mean in terms of the confusion between the big black Dicks of Jesus Christ & Shakespeare. And doesn't Ronald McDonald also have a big black Dick? Is it possible that Jesus Christ, Shakespeare, & Ronald McDonald are all the same person? Or perhaps they are different people who have used the same big black Dick? After all, they lived during different time periods, and therefore could have used the same big black Dick. This is what Henry Kissinger sitting on the toilet argues in an opinion piece in the Goop & More Goop Gazette. Here is a passage from that opinion piece:

"I feel myself Championing the cause of Shakespeare's big black Dick, because I really should Become a space alien in Brazil, but I keep getting shot with All these words, and this makes me Want to live 5000 years ago, but I really should Become a space alien in Brazil, because of all the Shakespeare big black Dick happening To me, but you see, it's so Déjà vu with lots of Ice cream!"

So, you see, Clones of Henry Kissinger sitting on the toilet are really Messengers from God! And if Endless-barking-dogs humping all the clones of Henry Kissinger sitting on the toilet are really A gift from God, then it stands to reason that

Shakespeare's big black Dick may be connected to Immaculate conception with the Virgin Mary. And if Shakespeare's Big black Dick is connected to Immaculate conception with the Virgin Mary, then one can deduce that We should all jump in active volcanoes, or What Cuckoo birds are running the world now? The dead bird on the sidewalk has studied this hypothesis scientifically at The Jacking Off Institute for the Special Studies of Activities Involving the Right Hand & the Penis. The dead bird on the sidewalk has come to the conclusion that Shakespeare ejaculated all of his plays all over the faces of English royalty out of his big black Dick. However, where's the proof? According to The dead bird on the sidewalk, the proof is in the Beautiful songs that Charles Manson sang with the

Beach boys. This idea is disputed by Your mother, who claims that Shakespeare's big black Dick must've come from Your father. Your mother argues that Kangaroos would make great politicians in his (Your mother changed genders five minutes ago) book "Why My Sons & Daughters Are A Different Species". Here is a passage from the S & M chapter of that book From your mother (who's now a man):

"All the buildings were hopping & skipping through a rat's brains, when the rat decided that He would take a ship to The other side of reality. This was very upsetting to Shakespeare's big black Dick, because of all the Pizza with Musical toppings. Of course, this goes to show you that The last century will jump over the next century to repeat history.

And that's why Shakespeare's big black Dick is So awesome!"

What Giant Euphoria Being bashed into your head With a sledgehammer! Or is this The cum you've been looking for? Of course, the argument here is whether Shakespeare was a space alien with a big black Dick, Or was Shakespeare a space alien with a small black Dick? Or, was Shakespeare a black man with a big space alien Dick, or was Shakespeare a black man with a small space alien Dick? Shedding light on this question is the studies of A cockroach crawling along your kitchen counter, who says: "The streets are rolling & rolling around in your insanity – watch out!" The two rats fornicating in your walls completely disagree with this, and The two rats say in unison: "We rats are having better sex than you do". Who is right?

To find the answer, we have decided to interview Shakespeare's big black Dick.

Wolf Larsen: "How much crazy you & crazy me?"

Shakespeare's big black Dick: "It all depends on the Size of the two planets of WOW hanging between your legs."

Wolf Larsen: "So I understand you've had sex with hundreds of homeless women, what's that like?"

Shakespeare's big black Dick: "It's like you're on the Titanic and it's sinking into a big stinky vagina."

Wolf Larsen: "What penis do you think goes best with white wine?"

Shakespeare's big black Dick: "I think you should ask Caligula that."

Wolf Larsen: "And finally, do you have any advice for any space aliens that may be reading this?"

Shakespeare's big black Dick: "You can write lots of poetry with your big black Dick."

Who's Afraid of Virginia Woolf's Nasty Pussy?

I was fucking my cat the other day – The kind with four legs & a tail – when my Cat told me: "If only I were bigger, I would be you!"

I responded to my cat: "I was kidnapped by a nAuGhTy-diShWaShiNg-mAcHiNe, And that's how I became an astronaut!"

Then Virginia Woolf crashed through the ceiling, and said: "You better give me my pussy back! Which one of you stole my pussy?"

That's when The Butt Fuck Army smashed down our door, and demanded to know: "Who's afraid of Virginia Woolf's nasty pussy?"

Immediately, a thousand scholars of Virginia Woolf's nasty pussy walked into the now open door of my studio apartment.

One of the thousands Of scholars in my studio apartment said as I continued to fuck my cat: "If you Fill Virginia Woolf's nasty puzzy With a college education, then Lots of flying seagulls will happen!"

Another scholar yelled out: "I did that once, and everything exploded with Words!"

And yet another scholar mysteriously whispered: "I'll sell you some Nasty pussy even nastier than Virginia Woolf's nasty Pussy!"

And then Virginia Woolf stuck her nasty pussy into my face and demanded that I eat it.

All the thousand scholars began chanting: "Eat that nasty pussy! Eat that nasty pussy! Eat that nasty pussy!"

I continued to fuck the cat while I ate Virginia Woolf's nasty pussy. While I ate Virginia Woolf's nasty pussy one of the thousands Of scholars in my studio apartment gave a learned speech on the nature of Virginia Woolf's nasty pussy:

"I was fucking some Garbage can, And then Extraterrestrial pussy happened, and I was so afraid because The Flying saucer full of midgets might find out, but then Virginia Woolf's nasty pussy Came to the rescue, and ever since then I've been hiding in the basement of your brains!"

What if this is really true? Does that intellectual discourse correctly describe the nature of Virginia Woolf's nasty pussy?

As someone that has personally eaten Virginia Woolf's nasty pussy, I can only say that The mermaids & Santa's elves fornicating inside the ballsack of a grizzly bear are very happy! Of course, as a Caucasian male, I have excellent pussy eating qualifications. Furthermore, I have a PhD in the art of eating pussy from the prestigious Ivy League Academy of Pussy Eating. And I can only say that eating Virginia Woolf's nasty pussy was a Religious experience.

Vladimir Putin, who also attended the prestigious Academy of Pussy Eating, is of the opinion that those who have eaten Virginia Woolf's nasty pussy are blessed with a truly intellectual experience, that is that the act of eating Virginia Woolf's nasty pussy is one of inTeLLecTuaL-niRvaNa-wOrmS. Vladimir Putin goes on to say:

"Take some Magical Elephants, and some Deadly Good looks, and then jump up and down like a Serial-killer-On-crack, and give yourself a brand-new Face, and then All the ducks in the pond will love you! And that's how you solve the economic crisis caused by Virginia Woolf's nasty pussy!"

Of course, not all students of Eating pussy agree with this Opinion. The Big Cucumber of the Pussy Eating College of Cannibalism, seems to feel that the rite of Nasty pussy eating is one of Ancient antiquity. I do not completely agree with this, because of Buildings hopping everywhere, but I also completely agree with this, because of Buildings hopping everywhere, and that is why drinking & more drinking & more drinking!, because after sticking my tongue into Virginia Woolf's nasty pussy I can only say that World War III tastes great!, and that is exactly why everyone should stick their tongues into Virginia Woolf's nasty pussy. Sharing this opinion that everyone should stick their tongue into Virginia Woolf's nasty pussy is A yeast infection, This yeast infection is a distinguished Professor of Around-and-Around at Yo-Yo University. The yeast infection states:

"It's totally Rivers-of-wine to say that Stormy skies taste great with Fried dinosaur brains! And that's why I feel So serial killer today! How do you feel? Do you feel the Irresistible temptation to tat-tat-tat & blam-blam-blam? Or do you feel like Masturbating? This has huge implications for the study of Virginia Woolf's nasty pussy, because of Itchy-itchy-itchy horny dogs, and also because of Car crashes, and let's not forget the Bountiful Semen of handsome strangers! So, Car crashes with lots of Virginia Woolf's nasty pussy!"

This is a very revolutionary doctrine! So let's grow giant forests of pubic hairs out of the walls of our studio apartments! And now for the Bombs-falling-through-air, as the intellectual basis of eating Virginia Woolf's nasty pussy, is at best very Lick-my-balls! Lick-my-balls! Lick-my-balls! Especially considering a Delicious pizza of Puppy & human flesh & Philosophy.

And then there are the differences between white & black scholars regarding performing cunnilingus on Virginia Woolf's nasty pussy. White scholars tend to believe that performing cunnilingus on the nasty pussy of Virginia Woolf is quite Heroic. Black scholars tend to believe the opposite, that performing cunnilingus on the nasty pussy of Virginia Woolf is Dangerous to Wildlife. Of course, these are generalizations. As there are some white scholars who believe that eating Virginia Woolf's nasty pussy is Their civic duty, and there are some black scholars who believe Lots-of-up-and-down with Spaghetti. Here to shed light on this question Is a bird in the tree, who is the Professor of Eating Nasty Pushy at the College of Erotic Cucumbers:

"Extraterrestrial jizz is The latest fashion in five-star haute cuisine, even if the boogers of our founding fathers are Sacred, and that's why Virginia Woolf's nasty pussy is Soon to be a saint in the Catholic Church."

This opinion is not shared by bourgeois feminists, who seem more concerned about supporting a woman president Bombing other countries, (As opposed to a male president bombing other countries), I mean Extraterrestrial snot, as many feminists are against women carrying a gun for self-defense, or Storm clouds drifting out of this page, as I myself the writer support free abortion on demand and I support free childcare and equal pay, but bourgeois feminists seem to think that the white man Sitting at the bus stop is some kind of "white male patriarchy", I mean what a bunch of Dancing ducks going quack quack quack! And of course, if you write an essay about Virginia Woolf's nasty pussy, then feminists think This must be some kind of Attila-the-Hun & His hordes of Oversexed Baboons Charging at Philosophy, which all seems very Incestuous Christmas. Here to shed light on this question is a Circus clown:

"The sexism of Lollipops, fornicating with a bunch of Stars in the sky, when you have liberal democratic-voting feminists who are every bit as uptight & puritanical as any Christian misogynistic religious fanatic then what the Sunrise? Both the feminists & the Christian religious fanatics want to censor everything with obscenity in it, so what's the Sunset?"

And this brings up the around-the-world question, what is the historical context Of Virginia Woolf's nasty pussy? NASA analyzed Virginia Woolf's nasty pussy from outer space. Joining this analysis with NASA is the very respected historian The Midnight Killer. This joint analysis by NASA & The Midnight Killer produced an outhouse full of Octopuses, or did it produce a Delicious chicken? That is the Baptize-my-bootyhole question! The Midnight Killer stated:

"Sometimes, with Circus clowns sliding around in your hair, And church bells going Bonkers with LSD, the mathematical equations cumming Out of Virginia Woolf's nasty pussy can be very Thunder & lightning, but if we understand the Psychedelic fish, and we consider the fish Tiptoeing into the Sky, then the Thunderstorms of Virginia Woolf's nasty pussy may actually accomplish world peace."

This historical analysis of Virginia Woolf's nasty pussy may actually contradict NASA's studies, or it may confirm NASA's studies, depending on the Horny wetness of Virginia Woolf's nasty pussy. NASA, when its rocketship blasted off into outer space, brought along a sample of Virginia Woolf's nasty pussy. That's when the space aliens took turns eating Virginia Woolf's nasty pussy. This first encounter between humans & extraterrestrials, thanks to Virginia Woolf's nasty pussy, is legendary. This legendary event involving Virginia Woolf's nasty pussy can only be considered Delicious. Or should it be considered French fries with a side of matricide? This is for the Easter Bunny to decide. The Easter bunnies of Satan sing together:

"We love the reader's Sweaty Testicles! And we love the reader's Buttocks! But we hate the reader's Eyeballs!"

One space alien, after eating Virginia Woolf's nasty pussy, exclaimed "Licorice!" Now, experts of Licorice-pussy-eating have been wondering why did the space alien say that, after eating Virginia Woolf's nasty pussy. Did the space alien say that because of Dandruff? Or were there Artificial intelligence civilizations of the future inside of Virginia Woolf's nasty pussy? What did Virginia Woolf's nasty pussy taste like to a space Alien?

Another historian of Virginia Woolf's nasty pussy, the Duke of Homelessness, considers space aliens eating Virginia Woolf's nasty pussy to be an adventure Of wild butterflies. But why? Did The

Duke of Homelessness think this because of a giant emptiness that was swallowing him?

Here to shed light on this is one of the space aliens that ate Virginia Woolf's nasty pussy, and who later founded the University of Eating Virginia Woolf's Nasty Pussy:

"I just so much Lost my brains, That I Be putting my Crazy poop with so much POP, and now I no have no Circus clowns to play me a Flying-Saucers-in-My-Stomach Orchestra, except when me Flying-saucer-titties Do lots of Delicious pizza with your Space alien pornography, you see the Space alien calligraphy all over the freight trains?"

However, there is something fishy here! Is it the smell of Virginia Woolf's nasty pussy? That would be too simple! What about the Wet dreams of sperm whales? And how do you explain the Whispers inside of Virginia Woolf's nasty pussy? This can only bring more questions, like the question of Voracious farm animals in my bed with me. In his book "A Thousand Questions About Virginia Woolf's Nasty Pussy", Professor Tits & More Tits & More Tits asks questions about Virginia Woolf's nasty pussy that are brilliant in their academic Cunnilingus with polar bears. Professor Tits & More Tits & More Tits even won the Plenty of Smelly Feet Prize for his outstanding work regarding all the plop-plop-plop in the toilet of questions about Virginia Woolf's nasty pussy. While copies of Professor Tits & More Tits & More Tits' book are quite rare, I was privileged enough to be mailed a copy by My favorite serial killer. I quote the following passage from Professor Tits & More Tits & More Tits' book "A Thousand Questions About Virginia Woolf's Nasty Pussy":

"Fireworks of genital warts below in the depths of Virginia Woolf's nasty pussy Occurs once every thousand years or so, depending on the Space alien invasions & the weather, and as a result The Milky Way Galaxy suddenly flies into your living room. To protect ourselves from the Volcanic eruptions of Virginia Woolf's nasty pussy, it is necessary for one to Masturbate for 24 hours a day, and to do so according to the Rules & Laws of The Sea of Insomnia, with the appropriate Chainsaw, because the Wild frontier of Virginia Woolf's nasty pussy can be very volatile with Hurricanes, especially considering lots of Howling dogs on days of Cannibalistic religions. So proper precautions of Jumping from a 100 story building are required when dealing with the Delicious pizzas flying out of Virginia Woolf's nasty pussy."

How invigorating! And how invigorating it is to study Virginia Woolf's nasty pussy. In fact, it has been known that studying Virginia Woolf's nasty pussy causes Hemorrhoids. Fantastic! It's so Otherworldly fantastic that All your ancestors just landed here from outer space!

Apparently, the founding fathers of the United States of America all had the chance to eat Virginia Woolf's nasty pussy. Benjamin Franklin, after eating Virginia Woolf's nasty pussy, is reported to have said:

"Regarding the authenticity of Virginia Woolf's nasty pussy, one's tongue inside the Armageddon of Virginia Woolf's nasty pussy will discover Lots of endangered species, and the Social services of one's tongue inside of Virginia Woolf's nasty pussy can accomplish great Catastrophes in the world! And that is why I recommend a thousand tongues inside of all the avant-garde architecture of Virginia Woolf's nasty pussy."

Also among those who have eaten Virginia Woolf's nasty pussy is the reader's dog. After eating Virginia Woolf's nasty pussy the reader's dog ran around the living room Hysterically a thousand times barking at all of the reader's insanity. Yet, why did the reader's dog react this way after eating Virginia Woolf's nasty pussy? Was it because of Fishbones in the Nasty pussy? Or was it because of Love in the Pubic hair regions of the Milky Way Galaxy? To answer this question of why the reader's dog reacted this way after eating the Virginia Woolf's nasty pussy is A cockroach crawling along the kitchen counter, who is the world renowned Author of the best-selling book "Eating Pussy for Nincompoops":

"It has come to my attention that Nasty pussy has Exponential qualities, and therefore when eating pussy it is important for the world to All clap together, Especially when all of the Sexually transmitted diseases are Waiting, and when the wet pussy is Flying into Everybody's imaginations, It is very important for Midgets with big dicks to Shout out obscenities to the Goddess of Four Letter Words. The accuracy of your Tongue inside of The Virginia Woolf's nasty pussy will determine whether North & South will reverse themselves and turn the planet

Earth upside down, or whether Smelly feet will Taste good. And now for the weather inside of Virginia Woolf's nasty pussy..."

This analysis is so Merry-go-round! What are we to think of this Syphilis of words? Of course, this Majority opinion of the Supreme Court is coming from somebody that Only recently ate out Virginia Woolf's nasty pussy. So what kind of Legal ruling from the Supreme Court regarding Virginia Woolf's nasty pussy do we expect? Of course, this kind of analysis may seem very up-the-river with lunatics, but actually it is quite Rocketship to the moon. This idea, so Disproven from all the pussy eating astronauts at NASA, is still believed today by some Dogs & Cats that live in Wolf Larsen's pubic hairs. But why? Perhaps it is because of the weather, or maybe It's because of Thoughts crawling all over the everything everywhere, or perhaps because of the Monsters in your shoes, but for whatever reason of Sunny days, this kind of cheap analysis of Virginia Woolf's nasty pussy is still believed by many. This Tragic misunderstanding of Virginia Woolf's nasty pussy is partially explained by Balloons in the air. Let us listen to the fine opinion of the Professor of Balloons-in-the-Air at the School of Somewhere Else:

"Trigger my Baloney sandwich! Anthropologists excavating Virginia Woolf's nasty pussy Have found ancient Roman ruins there! Dig your ears Into all the Bizarre hieroglyphics coming out of everybody's mouths! This nAstY-pUsSy-piE is so totally Delicious with Car races! We're all so Hyper with The Nasty Pussy

Extravaganza! Give us Sexually transmitted diseases, or give us a nuclear war!"

Unfortunately, this Full-of-vertigo diagnosis of Virginia Woolf's nasty pussy has not found its way to the eyes & ears of Prehistoric cavemen, and perhaps that is why My dry Itchy testicles are A God of Surprise. Or maybe, Global warming can explain this misunderstanding of Virginia Woolf's nasty pussy. That medieval scholars at monasteries hand copied so diligently This thoughtful discourse on Virginia Woolf's nasty pussy is why we are so profoundly educated on Virginia Woolf's nasty pussy today. Nonetheless, Cut out the Brains now! Furthermore, Onwards towards the Thoughts of My cat! And all I can say to that is, Check your Doo-Doo Privilege! Another opinion regarding the White privilege of Virginia Woolf's nasty pussy is A black nationalist's left testicle that lives on planet Mars. The left testicle of the black nationalist said:

"Regarding the white privilege of Virginia Woolf's nasty pussy one can only surmise that Waterfalls of Wizardry, except in cases of Eternal dizziness, when the Diarrhea is Delicious, and considering the tits of the Mona Lisa, it's quite possible that Space aliens live in your ears, but also quite impossible, Because of Buttocks sailing off to The funny farm, so it's important to Masturbate at all times."

And now for the Oatmeal cookies of Incestuous sex with your mother. Virginia Woolf's nasty pussy May not be Virginia Woolf's nasty pussy after all! Virginia Woolf's nasty pussy Might actually be a Fraud from One of the illegitimate children of Santa Claus. Or maybe, Virginia Woolf's nasty pussy might be a den of Alien beings. So, it is quite possible that Virginia Woolf's nasty pussy is only masquerading as Virginia Woolf's nasty pussy, And that's because Of Space stations growing out of everybody's head. This is a Naughty syndrome explained by Moons-in-the-sky Burning down, which is another syndrome explained by Faces-in-the-mirror burning down, which in turn is yet another syndrome explained by Space satellites In the toilet after a number two. Of course, all of this may seem rather Please-fuck-me-up-the-ass to the reader, yet there is lots of men-fucking-their-mothers to consider, especially when one is considering the validity of Virginia Woolf's nasty pussy.

The validity of Virginia Woolf's nasty pussy has been tested by the world's most foremost technicians. The conclusions of these technicians in nasty pussy eating have been debated for quite some time. The conclusions are mostly Full of cum, but sometimes Flavored with shit, and at other times rather Delicious. One technician who studied the Musical aspects of eating out Virginia Woolf's nasty pussy stated for the record:

"The musical aspects Of eating out Virginia Woolf's nasty pussy are so Delirious! So Yummy puppies everywhere! So pee on the Capitalist politicians & dictators, that you have to Sing-Snort-&-Sing again! This Trip across the Laziness of Mass Murdering is what we live for! That's why I study My buttocks in the library all day every day!

Now let's go eat some nasty pussy in honor of Virginia Woolf's nasty pussy!"

But then, something crazy happens! Virginia Woolf's nasty pussy is rumored to have said: "Eat me mother Fokker". But did Virginia Woolf's nasty pussy really say that? According to A homeless guy in the alley, Virginia Woolf's nasty pussy never said that because Cheap vodka is great! However, according to The reader's bunghole, Virginia Woolf's nasty pussy definitely said "Spit out that Warm sunny day Right now!" The reader's bunghole claims that Virginia Woolf's nasty pussy said this on holiday in Pre-history via Time Machine. However, this version of events is disputed by A screeching Meowing cat That's being stuffed into a meat grinder in my apartment right now. The screeching cat claims that "Virginia

Woolf's nasty pussy is a criminal organization stretching from The reader's testicles All the way to The planet of Pluto". However, I find this rather Hypnotizing . I mean, What happened to Chopping up cats and eating them?! And sometimes it appears that Virginia Woolf's nasty pussy was rather Gothic. This might appear to be rather Peanut-butter-on-the-moon, but is Virginia Woolf's nasty pussy schizophrenic? That is the question! A transsexual Albert Einstein of the Used Toilet Paper Institute for the Studies of Gobbledygook claims that:

"When we deduct Virginia Woolf's nasty pussy from the equation of Clouds-in-the-sky, and we add a bunch of cockle-doodle-dooooo in Boystown, and we multiply the cockle doodle dooooo's by 1,000 Gobbledygook monsters, we suddenly get Virginia Woolf's tits! That's Genius with Lots of delicious goldfish On top! And what's more, there's lots of gReaSy -uSeD-pUssY to go around."

This question of whether Virginia Woolf's nasty pussy was schizophrenic may be related to All the old alcoholic men I keep in my cellar for fun. After all, They don't make Space aliens like they used to! Studies regarding Space aliens seeking refuge inside of Virginia Woolf's nasty pussy have been conducted by Leonard Bernstein. Although the results of these studies were rather pornographic meatballs, these studies seem to indicate that Virginia Woolf's nasty pussy is Orbiting one of Jupiter's moons. But is Virginia Woolf's nasty pussy really Orbiting one of Jupiter's moons, or is Virginia Woolf's nasty pussy just pretending to orbit one of Jupiter's moons? That is the question that the experts of Watermelon have been asking for centuries. (Watermelon is soooo delicious!) The experts of watermelon eating & pussy eating at the Conference of Getting Drunk, have determined that:

"Whatever the church bells of Hell, and whatever the Sexy pigs-in-the-mud of Your favorite fairytale, people still need to know that Virginia Woolf's nasty pussy is a Temple of Tomorrow, And What is completely reassuring on this question of Talking tits, is the recurrence of Unidentified Flying Objects in all phenomena related to Virginia Woolf's nasty pussy, so we can all Breathe easier knowing that All our heads will be chopped off tomorrow!"

This is rather mysterious, especially if you are a Naked man wearing only a raincoat waiting on the street corner. Naked men Wearing only a raincoat consider Virginia Woolf's nasty pussy to be sacred, as in a religion of Give me money & more money & even more money glory hallelujah. The religion of Give me money & more money & even more money glory hallelujah considers Virginia Woolf's nasty pussy to be sacred because of Horny stray cats. However, this has been disputed by The local cat butcher, as Sarcastic storms are approaching. While this truth is routinely acknowledged, it must be stated that Virginia Woolf's nasty pussy is rather Outgoing. There is also lots of Wandering lizards to consider . Take for example, all the Howling animals in your testicles. All the Howling animals in your testicles Have been champions of Virginia Woolf's nasty pussy Ever since the reader died.

During the Napoleonic wars is when Virginia Woolf's nasty pussy became a champion In the Olympic Event of Eating Doo-Doo. As the champion of Eating Doo-Doo, everything is Sweet-Genocide-pie! Let us listen to Napoleon Bonaparte explain this doctrine:

"As Napoleon Bonaparte of This psychiatric ward, I feel that Virginia Woolf's nasty pussy has a Holistic meaning. Before I became Napoleon Bonaparte of This psychiatric ward, I was a Cloud in the sky, and that's when I knew Virginia Woolf's nasty pussy was rich in Antioxidants. Perhaps tomorrow when I become A squirrel in the park, I will have new Religious insights into the Holistic nature of Virginia Woolf's nasty pussy. I shall know when I wake up in the morning."

Anyway, the King of the Flying Saucers is Here! That's why the studies of Virginia Woolf's nasty pussy are so important to The Architects of Banana Peels. The Architects of Banana Peels have been debating the Physical & geographical properties of Virginia Woolf's nasty pussy since 1776. 1776 being the year that Virginia Woolf's nasty pussy Declared independence for the United States of America. And yet, what are we to make of the Spicy Aromas of Virginia Woolf's nasty pussy? Some regard the Spicy aromas of Virginia Woolf's nasty pussy as an occurrence of Ghostly visitations from Gothic movies. Others regard All of this Bouncing-eyeball-stuff as merely a hypothesis. Yet, what kind of hypothesis is this, if Virginia Woolf's nasty pussy is Conquering entire nations? Shedding light on this urgent question is A man talking to us from his photo in the Obituaries section of the newspaper, who states in his Report of Afterlife Sex that:

"Viewing Virginia Woolf's nasty pussy from the Orgies of the afterlife, I would have to say that I'm dead, but my penis is alive! Naturally Virginia Woolf's nasty pussy is an inspiration for all dead people. The dead people here in the afterlife are always telling me that Virginia Woolf's nasty pussy is their inspiration of pure love. An ancient Greek statue giving me a blow job was just telling me that Virginia Woolf's nasty pussy Helped him navigate the Seas of Dreams here in the afterlife. Sometimes, Virginia Woolf's nasty pussy visits us dead people in the afterlife, and Virginia Woolf's nasty pussy gives us inspirational speeches full of Flowers, for which we are so grateful!"

This is so Delicious-chopped up-neighbor that I can only say jibber-jabber! What are we to make of this Chocolate on my Dick? If Virginia Woolf's nasty pussy is as South side of Chicago as My anus says it is, then surely You got some delicious-licorice-sky For me! Yet, delicious-licorice-sky may merely be a manifestation of verbs cooking in the brain, considering the Dangerous monstrous bite of Virginia Woolf's nasty pussy. Except the Dangerous verbs cooking everywhere are sometimes considered a Frog-in-Wonderland, especially with all the siCk-gOrRiLLa-cHeeSe going around. And with all the Penises going around, one can only surmise that People are Hallucinating when they look in the mirror, because nobody exists. However, one should not assume that People are Made out of

Saturn's rings, merely because Virginia Woolf's nasty pussy is Eating out itself In outer space, So should we Eat ourselves out in outer space? In the Debates of Smelly Feet, your Favorite presidential Mass murderer stated:

"The musical celebrations inside of Virginia Woolf's nasty pussy are very Chocolatey with lots of LSD, and that's why I stand with the American people In applauding the Patriotism of Virginia Woolf's nasty pussy. And if I am elected as your President, I will give The Nasty pussy of Virginia Woolf a seat on my presidential cabinet, so help me God!"

You can literally Jump into outer space with this! The argument here is that Mysterious Civilizations of Four Letter Words is what defines Virginia Woolf's nasty pussy. Do you agree with this reader? If Mysterious Civilizations of Four Letter Words is what defines Virginia Woolf's nasty pussy, Then what about the Valleys & mountains & waterfalls In your closet? And what about the Oceans of Words splashing Around inside your head? The Splashing oceans of Virginia Woolf's nasty pussy is what creates Life on earth. Or is this a bunch of Cities & buildings & people falling out of space satellites? Anyway, The Prophets of Nasty Puzzy Eating have been admirers of Virginia Woolf's nasty pussy for centuries. Galileo, who studied Virginia Woolf's nasty pussy when it lived in outer space, well Galileo had this to say about Virginia Woolf's nasty pussy:

"Give me some Artificial intelligence Dick in-the-ass, because I gotta Find God, And I gotta Find the hole in the universe out of here, and I need a whole bunch of

Crazy words, in order to fix all these maladjustments in Virginia Woolf's nasty pussy. And I need a supersonic wrench to tighten all the Nuts & bolts of Virginia Woolf's nasty pussy. I also need The assistance of all the world's scientists in order to fix all the computer viruses that have infected Virginia Woolf's nasty pussy. You dig?"

Why did Galileo say This about Virginia Woolf's nasty pussy? Was it because of the Flood of Slobbering dog piss? Or was it because of the Earthquakes of Silly? The reader should consider the Earthquakes of Virginia Woolf's nasty pussy, because, after all, Subway trains and subway trains and subway trains, and what about Singing-Vibrators-saying-Howdy-do? Military historians have debated the effectiveness of Virginia Woolf's nasty pussy as a means of waging war against enemies. This Top Secret Information has come to us via satellite from Tarzan's hairy crotch, and may explain why armies have been using Virginia Woolf's nasty pussy as a weapon for centuries. Machiavelli even debated the effectiveness of Virginia Woolf's nasty pussy in palace intrigues during the Italian Anal Sex adventure in outer space. Commenting on the use of Virginia Woolf's nasty pussy in the Italian Anal Sex Adventure in outer space Machiavelli commented:

"You stick a bunch of Penis goo into the Presidential debates, and then you attach the Presidential debates To the 10,000 vaginas floating out of the Bible, and the Presidential debates you mix with a bunch of Horny German shepherds, and then you get Christmas! And that, my Boiling-pot-of-adjectives friend, will set

Virginia Woolf's nasty pussy off on the correct course into its voyage Into pre-Elizabethan literature."

When Machiavelli wrote this was he Smoking crack-cocaine with the President of the United States of America? Or was he Sitting on the toilet and flying off to The past or the future? A dog shitting in the park shed some light on this when he commented: "The Oversexed adjectives & Bizarre nouns & traveling verbs are coming!" Clearly, The dog shitting in the park and Machiavelli disagreed on the Ketchup & mustard & relish nature of Virginia Woolf's nasty pussy. Scientists have also debated this issue, as Virginia Woolf's nasty pussy has been a factor in interplanetary Herpes in the universe ever since Woodrow Wilson took a shit on national television. Yet, how did this come about? Did the Musical rhythms of Virginia Woolf's nasty pussy create nirvana on the moon? Or did All the symphonies & operas of Virginia Woolf's nasty pussy create Drive-by shootings instead? Who knows? But, perhaps A human corpse in a shallow grave in the forest preserve knows. The human corpse Is writing on the walls of a public toilet:

"Whatever the Crazy-crazy-crazy? And however the Now-now-now? Because if the universe is swallowed by Virginia Woolf's nasty pussy then what will we Eat for supper?"

When I encountered this on the walls of the public toilet, I knew instantly that Nuclear war was on the horizon, and that this Smelly Butthole Scholarship to study the Flying-about nature of Virginia Woolf's nasty pussy was a completely new development. But what kind of new development? Did this help shed light on the Airplanes & rocket ships that fly back-&-forth inside of Virginia Woolf's nasty pussy? Or was this wisdom on the walls of the public toilet really a confirmation of the stOrmY-wEaTheR-naTurE of Virginia Woolf's nasty pussy? During the Conference of Academic Diarrhea, A pig oinking-in-the-mud shed light on this public toilet wisdom when he said to an audience of professors of Toilet Wisdom:

"Something in the way she Shoots those Leprechauns with those Sweet bullets, makes me want to Vomit my happiness all over the Gray sky, but then I think of the Hairy Pussy Accomplishments of Virginia Woolf's nasty pussy, and I am inspired to pee all over the pUbLiShiNg-cOngLoMeRaTe-cOngLoMeRacY, and I think that Virginia Woolf's nasty pussy is a great inspiration to the human race, as This mountain is so very High with Hallucinations, which, I'm sure we can all agree!"

And this brings up the question, what is the future of Virginia Woolf's nasty pussy? While Virginia Woolf may be dead, Virginia Woolf's nasty pussy is alive & well with lots & Lots of feral cats! And that's why There's Lots of congressmen Up your nose. But if Virginia Woolf's nasty pussy is alive & well, then what is the prognosis for Circus clowns riding rocket ships to Your dinner table? And more importantly, what will future academic studies reveal about Virginia Woolf's nasty pussy?

An Interesting view on this question is held by A man imprisoned inside of your radio:

"Am I imprisoned inside of the reader's radio, or am I imprisoned inside of Virginia Woolf's nasty pussy? That is the question! And William Shakespeare is stuck here inside of Virginia Woolf's nasty pussy with me. It is the duty of the human race to free William Shakespeare & myself from the dungeon of Virginia Woolf's nasty pussy!"

So, is the future of Virginia Woolf's nasty pussy Written on the walls of the Egyptian pyramids? Or is the future of Virginia Woolf's nasty pussy Linked to global warming? What does the reader think? Does the reader think that Virginia Woolf's nasty pussy will cause a nuclear war? Or does the reader think that It would be nice to meet a nice sexy sheep? The decapitated head of Marie Antoinette seems to think that the future holds lots of Blue sky for Virginia Woolf's nasty pussy. Marie Antoinette's decapitated head said:

"Blue sky for Virginia Woolf's nasty pussy! Otherwise all the Continents of the world will Fall off the Earth! The future of Virginia Woolf's nasty pussy, and the future of mankind are linked together in a greatness of bLinking-on-&-Off-dildos And more bLinking-on-&-Off-dildos! And that is why I am proud that my decapitated head not only performed cunnilingus on Virginia Woolf's nasty pussy, but the cunnilingus of my decapitated head made Virginia Woolf's nasty pussy cum & cum & cuuuuuuuuuuuum!"

Disagreeing with Marie Antoinette's decapitated head is Your doorman. Your doorman seems to hold the opinion that the future of Virginia Woolf's nasty pussy is a bunch of Bologna sandwiches. However, this duddlie-do deduction can only be deduced by a bunch of Castrated dick sandwiches from Your favorite caveman, which may or may not be the opposite of the Christian values held by Virginia Woolf's nasty pussy. Virginia Woolf's nasty pussy itself said:

"The Christian values of nasty pussy has been around since Satan fucked Jesus up the ass, and that's why Virginia Woolf's nasty pussy is proud to present the reader with A magical rainbow! And it is an honor, As Virginia Woolf's nasty pussy, to receive the sperm of Wolf Larsen & Michelangelo & the Emperor of China & so many more distinguished citizens of our great whorehouse! And so, without further ado, I Virginia Woolf's nasty pussy announce that You can all Disappear! Thank you all, and God bless each and everyone of you with Lots of anal sex!"

So, the future of Virginia Woolf's nasty pussy may well be one of Intergalactic travel, And giving speeches to space aliens on the Wild-media-circus of other planets. However, scholars of Virginia Woolf's nasty pussy are still debating today whether the future of Virginia Woolf's nasty pussy is one of tornadoes or Earthquakes in your daily life. Perhaps the glorious future of Virginia Woolf's nasty pussy will be full of The reader's cum juices, or maybe Virginia Woolf's nasty pussy will be full of Nobel prize-winning philosophy, but one thing is for sure: I have to go jack off right now! I'm really horny!